The Tailor of Gloucester

The Tailor of Gloucester

FROM THE ORIGINAL MANUSCRIPT

WRITTEN AND ILLUSTRATED BY

Beatrix Potter

FREDERICK WARNE

LONDON AND NEW YORK

Published in Great Britain by
Frederick Warne & Co Ltd
London

Text and illustrations © Frederick Warne & Co Ltd 1969
Introduction © Leslie Linder 1969

Reprinted 1980

First published in the United States of America
Text and illustrations © Frederick Warne & Co Ltd 1968
Introduction © Leslie Linder 1968

LIBRARY OF CONGRESS CATALOG CARD NO 68 - 27844

ISBN 0 7232 1098 5

Printed in Great Britain by
Lowe & Brydone Printers Limited, Thetford, Norfolk
D6160.280

Introduction

It was during one of Beatrix Potter's visits to Harescombe Grange at Stroud, the home of her cousin Caroline Hutton, that she heard the story of the Tailor of Gloucester. Beatrix Potter tells how she 'had the story from Miss Caroline Hutton, who had it of Miss Lucy, of Gloucester, who had it of the tailor'. It was a strange story about a tailor who one Saturday had left in his shop a waistcoat, cut out, but not made up. The following Monday when he returned he found it finished except for one buttonhole, with a little scrap of paper pinned to the waistcoat, bearing the words 'no more twist'.

What had really happened was told many years later by Mrs. Prichard the tailor's wife. Every year there was a Root, Fruit and Grain Society Show at the Shire Hall, when the Mayor and City Corporation walked in procession from the Guildhall to the Show. The attending of this Function was the first duty of a new Mayor.

Mr. Prichard was on friendly terms with many of the Councillors, and on such occasions he was extremely busy. On this particular occasion he was so overwhelmed with orders that he even asked one of the Councillors if he could manage without his waistcoat so that he could make a very special one for the new Mayor. Work had been started on this special waistcoat: it was still unfinished and the Show was imminent—Mr. Pritchard was most concerned. When he left his shop that Saturday morning, the waistcoat was cut out and left lying on the board.

Mr. Prichard had two assistants who, realizing his concern about the waistcoat, and wishing to do their master a good turn, came back secretly to the shop that Saturday afternoon, letting themselves in with some skeleton keys. They worked on, until the waistcoat was finished—all but one button-hole—for they had run short of thread. They pinned a little note to the waistcoat bearing the words 'no more twist', and then went home as secretly as they had come.

When the tailor returned to the shop on Monday morning, he could hardly believe his eyes: there was the Mayor's waistcoat—finished—all but one button-hole. The two assistants said not a word, and the tailor was completely mystified. He brought the waistcoat down and put it in his shop-window, with a little sign by it which read 'Come to Pritchard where the waistcoats are made at night by the fairies'.

When Beatrix Potter heard this story she was intrigued—all her life she had been fascinated by the thought of fairies. Of her early childhood days at Dalguise in Scotland, she once wrote "Everything was romantic in my imagination. The woods were peopled by the mysterious good folk. The Lords and Ladies of the last Century walked with me along the overgrown paths in the garden". At once she felt that she must make this strange happening into a story. She would change the fairies into little mice, but the Mayor and the Tailor should remain true to life.

The next time Beatrix Potter was in Gloucester she made sketches of some of the streets and buildings, and of the archway into the precincts of the Cathedral. We are told how she sat on doorsteps in the streets of Gloucester in the hot, summer sunshine sketching *snowscenes* for her story. She also made background paintings of interiors of cottages in the neighbourhood, one of a bed with its hangings, another of a dresser complete with coloured crockery. At Harescombe Grange she painted the coachman's little boy sitting cross-legged on the floor posed as a tailor; also slumped in a chair in front of an imaginary fire.

Back in London Beatrix Potter needed some first-hand information about a tailor's workshop, so one day when she was walking past a tailor's shop in Chelsea, she pulled a button off her coat and went inside. While the tailor worked at this small repair she was able to have a good look at him, his tools and the snippets and odds and ends which surrounded him in his work-shop, and later made sketches of what she had seen. The tailor's shop was copied from a print of houses in old London city.

By December 1901 the story was finished, written out neatly in a stiff-covered exercise book, including twelve beautiful water-colours, based on some of the background sketches which Beatrix Potter had made—a Christmas present for Freda Moore, one of the little girls of her former governess. The note which accompanied the manuscript read:

Christmas 1901

My dear Freda,

Because you are fond of fairy-tales and have been ill, I have made you a story all for yourself—a new one that nobody has read before.

And the queerest thing about it—is that I heard it in Gloucestershire, and it is true! at least about the tailor, the waistcoat, and the 'No more twist'.

There ought to be more pictures towards the end, and they would have been the best ones; only Miss Potter was tired of it! Which was lazy of Miss Potter.

yrs. aff. H.B.P.

A year later Beatrix Potter decided that her story *The Tailor of Gloucester* should be privately printed: she had already borrowed the manuscript from Freda and made copies of the pictures. By December 1902, five hundred of the little books were ready—printed by Strangeways & Sons. She did not approach Frederick Warne & Co. who had just published her first book *The Tale of Peter Rabbit*, because, as she expressed it in a letter to Norman Warne—'I was quite sure in advance that you would cut out some of my favourite rhymes! which was one of the reasons why I printed it myself'.

What did Beatrix Potter think of the story? In a letter to Norman Warne, she wrote 'I will send you the little mouse book as soon as it is printed . . . Except the children's rough copy I have not showed it to anyone as I was rather afraid people might laugh at the words. I thought it a very pretty story when I heard it in the country, but it has proved rather beyond my capacity for working out . . . My opinion is that it is the best of them, but not as good as it ought to be': and in describing it to a friend she said 'I find that children of the right age—12—like it best; the smaller ones who could learn off the short sentences of *Peter* find this one too long.'

Fifteen years later it was still her favourite book, for she wrote in a presentation copy 'This is my favourite amongst the little books and I like this first edition because it contains more of the old rhymes . . .'

The book was seriously reviewed in an unexpected quarter— we are told by Beatrix Potter—"I have just been calling on my funny old tailor in Chelsea, and he said he had showed his copy to a traveller from the 'Tailor & Cutter', and told him about my drawing his shop, and they had put in a *beautiful* review!" The 'Tailor & Cutter' is the paper which the mouse on the bobbin is reading.

In the autumn of 1903, *The Tailor of Gloucester*, with fewer rhymes, but more illustrations, was published by Frederick Warne & Co. both in England and in the United States, and it is undoubtedly one of the outstanding children's books of the present Century.

Mr. Prichard the tailor, died in 1934, and his tombstone bears the inscription 'The Tailor of Gloucester'—a fine tribute from the City of Gloucester to the memory of the tailor, and an honour to Beatrix Potter the writer of this children's classic. It is gratifying to know that the original manuscript is permanently preserved in the Rare Book Department of the Free Library of Philadelphia.

Leslie Linder

Glossary

As many of the words used by Beatrix Potter in this original version are not in common use today, a glossary of these words with their definitions is included.

padusoy (paduasoy), n, *pad*-yew-soy, a corded silk material influenced by *Padua*

grey-beard mugs, n, *gray*-beard, large earthenware mugs

tobine, n, *toh*-bine, a stout twilled silk fabric

robins (for mice), n, *rob*-ins, a variant of 'robings'—meaning a trimming

throstle, n, *thros*-l, the song thrush

race (of ginger), n, race, a root (of ginger)

kyloe, n, *ky*-loh, one of a breed of small Highland black cattle

lutestring, n, *lewt*-string, a glossy silk fabric

taffeta, n, *taf*-e-ta, a material of flax and silk

pipkin, n, *pip*-kin, an earthen pot with a lid

ha'p'orth, n, *hay*-perth, halfpennyworth

After Hogarth.

In the time of swords and periwigs and full-skirted coats with flower'd lappets—when gentlemen wore ruffles and gold-laced waistcoats lined with padusoy or taffeta—there lived a tailor in Gloucester—

All day long while the light lasted, he sat cross-legged on a board in his booth on the south side of Westgate Street, sewing and snippetting, piecing out his velvet, and his silk of pink persian, and lutestring brocaded with thread of gold and silver. For stuffs had strange names and were very fine and expensive in the days of the tailor of Gloucester.

But though he sewed fine cloth for his customers he himself was very—very poor—a little old man with horn spectacles, a pinched face, crooked fingers, and a suit of threadbare clothes.

He sat on a table from morning till dark in the window of his booth, shaping and snipping and sewing; the floor below was all littered with with little scraps of silk, and snippets and ravellings— "They be too narrow measure for nought: except waist-coats—for mice—" said the tailor of Gloucester.

One day in December the snow clouds came down over Gloucester and it was early dark. The tailor worked and worked, and talked to himself excitedly. He was cutting out a coat and waistcoat for the Mayor of Gloucester—

A coat of cherry-coloured corded silk lined
with yellow padusoy, and a peach-coloured
waistcoat embroidered with rosebuds; and
both coat and waistcoat were worked about
the skirts and pocketholes with gold and
silver thread.

Said the tailor—

"I shall make my fortune—to be cut upon
the bias—the neck 19 inches—the chest
45—and 220 inches round the skirts of the
coat—to be ready by noon of Friday, the
25th day of December— Alack! I am worn to a
ravelling. But I shall make my fortune—
my money is all spent except one four-penny
bit— It shall have cherry-coloured buttonholes— But—alack!—I am undone, for I
have No More Twist—"

And still, while the tailor talked, he turned

the cloth about, and cut it with his shears,
and measured out silver braid and gold thread
and padusoy; and the floor was all covered
with cherry-coloured snippets.

When the snowflakes came down against
the small leaded windowpanes and shut out
the light, the tailor had cut out his work,
and all the separate pieces were spread upon
the table, ready to be sewn together in the
morning. There were twelve pieces of the coat,
and four pieces of the waistcoat—and also the
pocket flaps, the buttons and the lining—all
were laid in order. The silver braid and gold
thread were measured out—nothing was
wanting, but just one single skein of cherry-
coloured twisted silk.

The tailor locked up his booth and put
the key in his pocket, and shuffled home

through the snow, to the kitchen-cellar
where he lived, with his cat. (It was called
Simpkin).

All the way up Westgate, and down the
lane—called Three Cocks' Lane—and down
the cellar steps he shuffled, mumbling to
himself about the Mayor of Gloucester and
the coat of cherry-coloured corded silk. He
knocked at his door, and it was opened by
Simpkin, who said. "Miaw?" The tailor
replied—

"Simpkin! we shall make our fortune; but
I am worn to a ravelling. Simpkin, take this
groat which is our last four-pence, and Simpkin,
take a pipkin; buy a penn'orth of milk, a
penn'orth of bread and a penn'orth of
sausages, and O Simpkin! with the last
penny of our four-pence buy me one penn'orth

of cherry-coloured twist. The Mayor of
Gloucester shall be married on Christmas Day
in the morning, and he hath ordered a coat
and an embroidered waistcoat. We shall make
our fortune. But lose not the last penny of
the four-pence, Simpkin, or I am undone, and
worn to a thread-paper; for I have NO MORE
TWIST!"

Then Simpkin said "Miaw?" and took the
groat and the pipkin.

The tailor was very tired and cold, and
although he did not know it, he was
beginning to be ill.

He sat close over the hearth and warmed his
hands, and swayed about upon his stool,
mumbling, and talking about that wonderful
coat—

"I shall make my fortune: but alack, I am

worn to a ravelling . . . to be ready by noon of Friday . . . and this is Monday . . . cut bias . . . It shall be lined with yellow padusoy, and laced with silver thread about the pocket flaps. . . . Shaped and planned and cut bias . . . . . and the padusoy sufficeth; there is no more left over in snippets than will make waistcoats for mice. . . . Was I wise to entrust my last penny to Simpkin? Alack, I am undone, for I have no more twist!"

Then the tailor started, for suddenly interrupting him, from the dresser at the other side of the kitchen came a row of little noises—

Tap tap: tap tap: tap tap, tip!

"Now what may that be?" said the tailor of Gloucester.

B

The dresser was covered with cracked plates and crockery, and pie-dishes and pipkins, and grey-beard mugs and pewter plates—

The tailor stepped across the tiled floor of the kitchen; and again from under a tea-cup came the little sounds—

Tip tap: tip tap: tap tap tip!

"This is very peculiar!" said the tailor of Gloucester, and he lifted a tea-cup which was upside down.

Out stepped a little live lady-mouse, and made a low curtsey to the tailor!

Then she hopped away down off the dresser
and under the wainscot—

The tailor sat down again on his three-legged
stool, and talked to himself, and warmed his
cold hands— "The waistcoat is cut out from
peach-coloured satin, and gold thread
embroidery is worked about the edge. The
braid and the fringe is of gold and silver
thread . . . tobine stripes and rosebuds in
beautiful floss silk . . . the thread is cut and
measured and everything sufficeth . . . there
is no more left in snippets than will make
robins for mice . . . but— Alack! I am undone,

for I have no more twist! . . ." Then all at once from the dresser came a chorus of little tip-taps, all sounding together and answering one another, like watch-beetles in old worm-eaten window shutters—

Tap tap: tap tap: tap tap tip!

"This is passing extraordinary!" said the tailor of Gloucester.

He lifted two more tea-cups and a bowl and a basin, and the lid of the tea-pot and two or three mugs.

Out from under each came little live gentlemen mice, and made bows to the tailor.

Then they hopped away down off the dresser, and under the wainscot.

The tailor sat down again by the fire and rubbed his poor cold hands, and mumbled to himself about the Mayor of Gloucester and the cherry-coloured coat—

"The pocketholes are set about with thread of gold embroidery, and much of it is worked upon the skirts of the coat . . . the skirts shall be stiffened with whalebone and horse-hair . . . one and twenty buttonholes of cherry-coloured twist! . . . Have I done well in entrusting my last penny to Simpkin? . . . Well-a-day! I am worn to a shred and a thread-paper! Was I wise to enfranchise those mice; undoubtedly the property of Simpkin? Alack, I am undone; for I have no more twist!"

But all at once interrupting him came a chorus of little tip taps; from the wainscot and the floor and the chimney and from under the four-post bed in the corner—

Tip tap: tap tap: tip tap tip!

Then a came a louder knock— Rat-tat-tat!— upon the house-door, and the little noises ceased.

The tailor opened the door, and in bounced Simpkin, with a whirl of snowflakes and an angry

"Miaw grrr ruck!" like a cat that is vexed—his coat was scrumpled up at the back of his neck; there was snow in his ears, and snow upon the milk in the pipkin.

"Simpkin" said the tailor, "*where is my twist?*"

But Simpkin set down the pipkin and the bread upon the dresser, and sniffed.

"Simpkin' said the tailor, *where is my twist?*"

But Simpkin set down the sausages on a plate upon the dresser, and turned about bowls and the basins and sniffed.

"Alack, I am undone," said the tailor of Gloucester.

"Miaw grrruck!" said Simpkin. He slipped a little packet into the tea-pot, and looked angrily at the tailor—

"Grrr miaw!" said Simpkin, as he turned over the plates.

All night long the wind howled and whistled; it drifted the snowflakes under the door.

The tailor tossed and turned in his four-post bed in the corner of the kitchen, and still in his dreams he mumbled:

"No more twist!"

The windows rattled and the wind roared in the chimney; and all through the night Simpkin wandered about, searching the kitchen from ceiling to floor—

He peeped under tea-cups and turned over basins, he mewed and hunted and sniffed; he looked into cupboards and under the wainscot.

Whenever the tailor spoke in his sleep, Simpkin said "Miaw? gerrrrwsssch!!" and made strange horrid noises like cats do at nights.

When the sun rose next morning, like a red ball over the plain, the snow was lying deep in all the streets of Gloucester.

It had drifted about the steep roof and attic windows and all about the College green and the Cathedral towers. Down by the wharfs the masts of the ships showed black against the snow: all the vale of Severn and the hills on either hand were covered with a great white sheet.

In the narrow streets folks shovelled and
scraped and dug out their doorways, whistling
as they worked. The shovels made a cheerful
clink clink upon the stones, and the jackdaws
from the Cathedral came down where the
snow was cleared. They ran about with their
heads on one side, turning in their toes, and
fighting for scraps of bacon outside the
Mayor of Gloucester's shop—
[For the Mayor was a grocer, at the Sign of
the Golden Candle, at the corner of Westgate
and Three Cocks' Lane.]
But no one came near the little booth where
the Mayor of Gloucester's fine Christmas
clothes lay spread out upon the table.

There were ten pieces of the coat besides the cuffs, and the waistcoat; all lay ready in order, but there was no one to sew them.

For the poor old tailor lay upon his four-post bed very ill with a fever, and all the time he tossed and turned he mumbled "No more twist, no more twist!"

And Simpkin said "Mew?" and stood beside the bed.

All that day he was ill; and the next day and the next; and what should become of the cherry-coloured coat? And when the bread should be finished, and the milk in the pipkin— what would become of Simpkin and the tailor?

Three days the tailor tossed and turned and Simpkin mewed and walked backwards and forwards over the bed; and still the tailor mumbled about cherry-coloured twist.

And Simpkin grew thin and anxious, and mewed more and more piteously.

Out of doors it was Christmas Eve, and folks were trudging through the snow to buy their geese and turkeys and bake their Christmas pies.

But it looked as though there would be no
Christmas dinner for Simpkin, and the poor
old tailor of Gloucester.

In the evening the big round face of the
moon climbed up over the roof and peeped
down into the kitchen-cellar, where the fire
had gone out, and there was very little left
to eat—except mugs and pewter plates—

Late at night upon Christmas Eve Simpkin
opened the door and went out, up the cellar

steps. He jumped nimbly over the snow in the gutter and crossed into the shadow over the way. On the side of the street where the moonlight fell, the icicles sparkled like diamonds; the overhanging gables and little lattice windows showed quite plain; although it was the middle of the night. There were no lights in the windows and no sounds in the houses, everyone had gone to bed. Only in the distance—fainter and fainter a long way off— the carol singers were singing an old Christmas tune—

"Wassal, wassal, to our town!
  The cup is white and the ale is brown;
  The cup is made of the ashen tree,
  And so is the ale of the good barley.

"Little maid, little maid, turn the pin,
  Open the door and let us come in!

"Blessed be the master of this house, and the
      mistress also,
  And all the little babies that round the table
      grow!
  Their pockets full of money, the cellars full of
      beer—
  A merry Christmas to you, and a happy New
      Year!"

The merry voices died away in the distance; the waits and carol singers too had gone to bed.

All the city of Gloucester was fast asleep.

Up and down and round about, all round the town went Simpkin.

He sniffed about the gutters and searched amongst the snow.

He wandered through the market-place; but all the Christmas beef was sold; not a scrap of suet or a single old bone was left under the stalls. The jackdaws had been hungry too; and they had been there before poor Simpkin.

Simpkin went to look whether they had dropped anything on their way home; he crossed the smooth white snow in the College gardens leaving a row of round pit-pats to mark his track. There was not a sound; it was so very very quiet, that Simpkin scarcely liked to mew.

Then all at once up above his head there was a sort of buzzing sound of wheels, and the Cathedral clock began to strike the chimes. Such a merry jingling noise of bells echoing over the snow!

The jackdaws woke, and all began to shout together, and all the cocks in Gloucester began to crow.

Although it was the middle of the night, the throstles and the robins sang in the College

C

gardens; before the last echo of the chimes had gone—the air was quite full of little twittering voices talking altogether! Even poor hungry Simpkin looked up at the moon, and sighed—

"Hey diddle diddle!" For it is in the old story, that all the beasts can talk in the night between Christmas Eve and Christmas Day in the morning—

But there are very few folks that can hear them, or know what they say.

From all the gardens and roofs and cellars and old wooden houses in Gloucester came thousands of little twittering voices, singing the old Christmas rhymes.

All the old songs that ever I heard of; and some that I don't know—like "Whittington's Bells."

First and loudest the cocks sang out—

> *"Dame get up and bake your pies,*
>   *Bake your pies! bake your pies!*
> *Dame get up and bake your pies,*
>   *On Christmas Day in the morning."*

Cock a doodle doo! shouted the cocks; Then they sang another verse—

> *"Dame what makes your maidens lie?*
>   *Maidens lie, maidens lie,*
> *Dame what makes your maidens lie*
>   *On Christmas Day in the morning."*

Cock a doodle doo! Cock a doodle doo!
shouted the cocks.

"Hey diddle, diddle!" sighed Simpkin. Then
the cocks sang the last two verses—

> *"Dame, what makes your ducks to die?*
> *Ducks to die, ducks to die,*
> *Dame what makes your ducks to die?*
> *On Christmas day in the morning."*

> *"Their wings are cut, and they cannot fly,*
> *Cannot fly, cannot fly,*
> *Their wings are cut and they cannot fly,*
> *On Christmas day in the morning."*

"Oh dilly dilly dilly!" sighed the hungry
Simpkin, "Oh what shall we have for supper,
Mrs. Bond? . . . There's geese in the larder and
ducks in the pond! But my master's larder is as
empty as old Mother Hubbard's," sighed

Simpkin—And the Mayor's little turnspit doggie overhearing him took up the song—

> *"When she got there,*
> *The cupboard was bare,*
> *And so the poor doggie had none!"*

It was in the stable yard taking supper with the watchdog; they looked up at the moon and laughed until they cried—

The turnspit began another tune—

> *"I had a little dog,*
> *And they called him Buff!*
> *I sent him to the shop*
> *For a ha'p'orth of snuff;*
> *But he lost the bag,*
> *And spill'd the snuff,*
> *So take that cuff!*
> *And that's enough."*

Inside the stables the fat horses moved in
their stalls and jingled the chains and rings—

> *"John Smith*
>   *Fellow fine*
> *Can you shoe this horse of mine?*
>   *Yes Sir that I can,*
>   *As well as any man,*
> *Here a nail and here a prod,*
> *Now the horse is well shod."*

"Ride a cock-horse to Banbury Cross."
grumbled Simpkin.

He went up Westgate and looked up at the
funny old houses with their carved gables and

painted sign boards hanging out in the moonlight. In a garret in the roof of the Sun Inn
there were lights and the sound of fiddling—

> *"Old King Cole, was a merry old soul,*
> *And a merry old soul was he,*
> *He called for his pipe*
>   *And he called for his bowl,*
> *And he called for his fiddlers three—*
>
> *Fiddle fiddle fiddle!*
>   *went the fiddlers three,*
> *Fiddle, fiddle, fiddle, fiddle, fee!*
> *Oh there's none so rare*
>   *As can compare*
>   *With King Cole and his fiddlers three!"*

"Hey diddle, diddle! The cat and the fiddle! All the cats in Gloucester, except me," sighed Simpkin.

In the cellars under the Mayor of Gloucester's shop, at the Sign of the Golden Candle, where Simpkin had bought the sausages—there was a fine racket! The rats were holding holiday and highjinks, singing the song of "Uncle Rottan," and dancing the hays, in and out and round about, amongst the casks and barrels. Thumpetty, bumpetty, bump, they danced, and then came shrieks of laughter and a crash of broken bottles—

Simpkin, with his ears and tail jerking,
listened close against a chink in the trap-door,
while a squeaky voice sang this ancient ditty—
(for they were old English black rats; the
gray rats had not come from Norway in the
days of cherry-coloured coats).

Sang the squeaky voice—

"It was the frog liv'd in a well,
Kitty alone, Kitty alone,
And a merry mouse in a mill—
Cock me cary, Kitty alone,
Kitty alone, and I—"
(Thumpetty bumpetty bump, danced the
rats)—

"When he was on his high horse set,
  His boots they shone as black as jet,
    Cock me cary, Kitty alone,
      Kitty alone and I.
"When he came to the merry mill pin,
  'Lady Mouse, are you therein?'
      Kitty alone, Kitty alone!"

(Simpkin grinned.)

"Then out came the dousty mouse,
  'I'm my lady of this house.
  Softly do I sit and spin—'
      Kitty alone, Kitty alone—"

"Mistress Mouse, I'm come to thee,
To see if thou cans't fancy me?
Cock me cary, Kitty alone,
    Kitty alone, and I."

"Marriage can I grant you none,
 Till Uncle Rottan he comes home,
    Kitty alone, Kitty alone."

" 'What shall we have to our supper?'
 'Three beans and one pound of butter.'
   Cock me cary, Kitty alone,
    Kitty alone, and I."

"Lord Rottan sat at head o'th'table,
  Because he was both stout and able—"

"Miaw Miaw! cried Simpkin very loud at
the trap-door.

There was an interruption and more
smashing of glass—

Presently the rude squeaky voice began
again, close to his ear on the other side of the
door—

"Then did come in Gib our cat,
  With a fiddle on his back,
  —Want you any music here"—

Gggrrr miaw! cried Simpkin—

"The cat he pull'd Lord Rottan down,
  The kittlins they did claw his crown—
Cock me cary, Kitty alone.
  Kitty alone and I—"

It was too offensive: Simpkin did not wait to hear any more; except that he could not avoid overhearing echoes of the tune of "Aikin Drum" which all the rats sang loudly in chorus—

> *"And he ate up all the good roast beef,*
> *The good roast beef,*
> *The good roast beef,*
> *And he ate up all the good fat tripe,*
> *The good fat tripe,*
> *The good fat tripe,*
> *And his name was Aikin Drum!*
> *And he played upon a ladle,*
> *With a fi fee feedle fum!"*

Simpkin hurried away out of hearing of that
disreputable company in the Mayor of
Gloucester's cellar—

He went up Westgate and listened to some
much prettier singing; for the air was quite
full of little tunes, and twittering voices—

Under the wooden eaves the sparrows sang in
their sleep—

> *"Intery, mintery, cuttery corn!*
> *Apple seed, and apple thorn!"*

Then another little voice from over the way—

> "*Upstairs and downstairs,*
> *Upon my lady's window,*
> *There I saw a cup of sack,*
> *And a race of ginger!—*"

And another sang

> "*I had a little nut tree,*
> *Nothing would it bear,*
> *But a golden nutmeg,*
> *And a silver pear,*
> *The King of Spain's daughter*
> *Came to visit me,*
> *And all for the sake of*
> *My little nut tree!*"

And then another began to sing about Little Jack Horner and Christmas pies; but another little bird interrupted him with—

> *"Little Poll Parrot*
> *Sat in a garret*
> *Eating toast and tea!*
> *A little brown mouse,*
> *Jumped into his house,*
> *And stole it all away!"*

And then they all sang together from both
sides of the street—

> *"Once I saw a little bird*
> *Come hop, hop, hop!*
> *So I cried 'Little bird,*
> *Will you stop stop stop?'*
> *And was going to the window*
> *To say 'how do you do?'*
> *But he shook his little tail,*
> *And away he flew!"*

D

From the tailor's little booth in Westgate came a gleam of light. When Simpkin crept up to peep in at the window it was full of candles.

There was a snippetting of scissors, and click of thimbles and snappetting of threads.

Little mouse voices sang loudly in chorus—

"Four and twenty tailors went to catch a snail,
  The best man amongst them
  Durst not touch her tail;
  She put out her horns
  Like a little kyloe cow,
  Run, tailors run! or she'll kill you all e'en
      now!"

Then without a pause the little mouse voices went on again gaily—

> "*Sieve my lady's oatmeal,*
> *Grind my lady's flour,*
> *Put it in a chestnut,*
> *Let it stand an hour;*
> *One may—*"

Mew! Mew! interrupted Simpkin.

The little mouse voices tried another tune—

"Can you make me a cambric shirt,
—Parsley, sage, rosemary and thyme—
Without any seam or needle work?
And you shall be a true lover of mine."

"Mew? mew?" cried Simpkin at the keyhole.

The little voices struck into a very brisk measure—

"Hey diddle dinketty, poppety pet!
The merchants of London they wear scarlet;
Silk in the collar, and gold in the hem,
So merrily march the merchant men!"

"Miaw! cried Simpkin, "Miaw!

The little voices tittered and began again—

> *"Jack Sprat*
>   *Had a cat,*
> *It had but one ear;*
>   *It went to buy butter,*
> *When butter was dear—"*

"Miaw! ggrrrr! cried the exasperated Simpkin under the door—but the little voices tittered and began again—

> "*And there I bought*
> *A pipkin and a popkin,*
> *A slipkin and a slopkin,*
> *All for one farthing—*
> *And upon the kitchen dresser!*"

added the little tittering voices.

'Ggrrrr miaw! cried Simpkin. Then they began again a most lively jingle, snippetting their scissors to mark time—

> *"Hark! hark!*
>   *The dogs do bark,*
> *The Beggars are come to town,*
>   *Some in tags*
>   *And some in rags*
> *And one in a velvet gown!"*

"Ggrrrr miaw!" cried Simpkin.

The little voices tittered—

> *"Pussy-cat Mole,*
>   *Jump'd over a coal,*
> *And in her best petticoat*
> *burnt a great hole*
> *Poor Pussy's weeping,*
> *She'll have no more milk,*
> *Till her best petticoat's*
> *Mended with silk!"*

"Miaw! scratch, scratch!" scuffled Simpkin
jumping onto the window sill, while the little
mice inside sprang to their feet and sang
altogether—

> *"Three little mice sat down to spin!*
>   *Pussy pass'd by and she peeped in.*
> *'What are you at my fine little men?'*
> *"Making coats for Gentlemen!"*
> *'Shall I come in and cut off your threads?'*
> *"Oh NO! Miss Pussy; you'd bite off our*
>   *heads!"*

And then they all began shouting at once in little twittering voices "No more twist! no more twist! No more twist!" and they barred up the window shutters, and shut out Simkpin.

But still through the nicks in the shutters he could hear the click of thimbles and little mouse voices singing "No more twist! No more twist!"

Simpkin came away home to the kitchen-cellar, considering thoughtfully in his mind.

When he opened the door and went in, he found that the poor old tailor was fast asleep! The fever had left him. Then Simpkin went on tip-toe to the kitchen dresser, and took a little parcel out of the tea-pot, and looked at it in the moonlight.

When the tailor awoke in the morning the first thing he saw—upon the patch work counterpane—was a skein of cherry-coloured twisted silk. Beside his bed stood the repentant Simpkin with a cup of tea and the last of the sausages, fizzling hot upon a pewter plate.

"Alack, I am worn to a ravelling," said the tailor of Gloucester, "but I have my twist!"

Out of doors the sun was shining on the snow and the bells rang merrily.

The tailor got up and hobbled along the sunny side of the way with Simpkin running at his heels or before him; and when the tailor lagged, Simpkin ran in front before him, and mewed, like a cat in a hurry. The robins and throstles sang, and the sparrows and starlings twittered and whistled upon the chimney stacks. And the carol singers too had come out again—for folks seem to have sung at all manner of times, in the days of cherry-coloured coats—and this was what they sang—

"I saw three ships come sailing by—
  Sailing by, sailing by,
 I saw three ships come sailing by—
 On Christmas Day in the morning.

And who do you think were in them then?
  In them then, in them then,
And who do you think were in them then?
On Christmas Day in the morning!

Three pretty maids were in them then—
  In them then, in them then,
 Three pretty maids were in them then—
 On Christmas Day in the morning.

One could whistle, and one could sing,
  And one could play on the violin,
Such joy was at my wedding
On Christmas Day in the morning!"

Said the tailor—

"Alack, I have my twist, but no more strength—nor time—than will make me one single button-hole—and this is Christmas Day in the morning! The Mayor of Gloucester shall be married at noon; and where is his cherry-coloured coat?"

He fitted the key into the lock of his booth with a shaky hand; and Simpkin ran in, between his legs like a cat that expects something—

"Mew? Mew?" cried Simpkin.

But there was no one there—

The floor was swept and clean; the pins were all swept up and stuck into pin papers; the ends of thread and little silk snippets were all tidied away, and gone from the floor.

But upon the table! Oh joy—the tailor gave a shout!

There—where he had left plain cuttings of cloth—there lay the most beautifullest coat and gold-brocaded waistcoat that ever were worn by a mayor of Gloucester.

There was embroidery upon the cuffs and upon the pocket flaps and upon the skirts of the coat: it was cherry-coloured corded silk, lined with yellow padusoy; there were one-and-twenty buttons.

The waistcoat was of peach-coloured satin, worked with thread of gold and silver.

Everything was quite finished except just one
single cherry-coloured buttonhole; and where
that buttonhole was wanting, there was pinned
a little scrap of paper, with these words—in
teeny weeny writing—

"no more twist":

And from then began the luck of the tailor
of Gloucester; he grew quite stout and he grew
quite rich.

He made the most wonderful waistcoats for
all the rich merchants of Gloucester, and for
all the fine gentlemen of the country round—

Never were seen such lappets and such cuffs
and such tabby silks and rosebuds!

But his buttonholes were the greatest
triumph of all.

The stitches were so neat—so neat—I wonder how they could be made by a little old man in spectacles, with old crooked fingers, and a thimble on his thumb!

The stitches of those buttonholes were so small—so small—they looked as if they had been stitched by little mice!